Your Reading Log

A Reading Journal to Record Your Impressions from Books You Have Read

Page designer: Leda Vaneva

ISBN No. 978-1632871343

Spirala Publishing

Spirala Journals

Spirala Publishing

Spirala Publishing
contact@spiralaPublishing.com
www.spiralaPublishing.com

Publisher's Note: This is a work of fiction. Names, characters, places, and incidents are a product of the author's imagination. Locales and public names are sometimes used for atmospheric purposes. Any resemblance to actual people, living or dead, or to businesses, companies, events, institutions, or locales is completely coincidental.

Ordering Information:
Quantity sales. Special discounts are available on quantity purchases by corporations, associations, and others. For details, contact the "Special Sales Department" at the address above.

Spirala Journals / Your Reading Log: a Reading Journal to Records your Impressions from Books you have Read - 1st ed.
ISBN 978-1632871343

Distributed by:
Speedy Publishing LLC
40 E. Main St. #1156
Newark, DE 19711
www.speedypublishing.co

How to use this Journal?

Congratulations on purchasing a journal from the Spirala Journals collection. We know that in today's fast paced world, keeping track of what one loves and enjoys can be quite a challenge. With our busy lifestyles and the proliferation of digital modes of entertainment, keeping one's passion for books and reading is something that is usually taken for granted. We developed this reading log as a part of our Spirala Journals collection to give you an outlet to write about the books that you've read and, thus, help in preserving the love of the written word.

With our special journals from the Spirala Journals collection, having an easy to use book journal for both reading neophytes and reading veterans is made more enjoyable. You may use this reading log as a personal record or perhaps as a comprehensive note-taking tool for books that you would want to share.

With your purchase of our journal, Your Reading Log, you can record what titles you have read together with other important book details such as author name and your rating for the book. This gives you a complete record of every single book you have read and your thoughts about the book which you can review and appreciate years down the road.

For the best use of the journal, Your Reading Log, we recommend the following actions:

1. Keep your reading journal near you or place it on your favorite reading nook.
2. Make sure to note the date you started reading the book and the date you finished it.
3. Rate the book which you've read to serve as a guide in case you would like to recommend certain books in the future to a fellow bookworm.
4. Write the ideas about the book that left a mark on you and prompted you to explore more. These are great ideas for picking out which titles to read next.
5. Share your reading journal to fellow book lovers!

Your Reading Log book journal serves as a great tool, which affirms your love of books. Think of it as a mini review of the books that you liked or have read. It is through the flame of the written word that the best ideas are conveyed, touching people with thoughts and ideas that transcend distance and time. Cheers to being a book warrior!

Book title

Author

Date started

Date finished

Genre

Rating ☆ ☆ ☆ ☆ ☆

Passages, quotes and ideas to remember

Made me want to learn more about these subjects

Book title

Author

Date started

Date finished

Genre

Rating ☆ ☆ ☆ ☆ ☆

Passages, quotes and ideas to remember

Made me want to learn more about these subjects

Book title

Author

Date started

Date finished

Genre

Rating ☆☆☆☆☆

Passages, quotes and ideas to remember

Made me want to learn more about these subjects

Book title

Author

Date started

Date finished

Genre

Rating ☆ ☆ ☆ ☆ ☆

Passages, quotes and ideas to remember

Made me want to learn more about these subjects

Book title

Author

Date started

Date finished

Genre

Rating ☆☆☆☆☆

Passages, quotes and ideas to remember

Made me want to learn more about these subjects

Book title

Author

Date started

Date finished

Genre

Rating ☆☆☆☆☆

Passages, quotes and ideas to remember

Made me want to learn more about these subjects

Book title

Author

Date started

Date finished

Genre

Rating ☆ ☆ ☆ ☆ ☆

Passages, quotes and ideas to remember

Made me want to learn more about these subjects

Book title

Author

Date started

Date finished

Genre

Rating ☆ ☆ ☆ ☆ ☆

Passages, quotes and ideas to remember

Made me want to learn more about these subjects

Book title

Author

Date started

Date finished

Genre

Rating ☆☆☆☆☆

Passages, quotes and ideas to remember

Made me want to learn more about these subjects

Book title

Author

Date started

Date finished

Genre

Rating ☆ ☆ ☆ ☆ ☆

Passages, quotes and ideas to remember

Made me want to learn more about these subjects

Book title

Author

Date started

Date finished

Genre

Rating ☆ ☆ ☆ ☆ ☆

Passages, quotes and ideas to remember

Made me want to learn more about these subjects

Book title

Author

Date started

Date finished

Genre

Rating ☆ ☆ ☆ ☆ ☆

Passages, quotes and ideas to remember

Made me want to learn more about these subjects

Book title

Author

Date started

Date finished

Genre

Rating ☆ ☆ ☆ ☆ ☆

Passages, quotes and ideas to remember

Made me want to learn more about these subjects

Book title

Author

Date started

Date finished

Genre

Rating ☆☆☆☆☆

Passages, quotes and ideas to remember

Made me want to learn more about these subjects

Book title

Author

Date started

Date finished

Genre

Rating ☆ ☆ ☆ ☆ ☆

Passages, quotes and ideas to remember

Made me want to learn more about these subjects

Book title

Author

Date started

Date finished

Genre

Rating ☆☆☆☆☆

Passages, quotes and ideas to remember

Made me want to learn more about these subjects

Book title

Author

Date started

Date finished

Genre

Rating ☆☆☆☆☆

Passages, quotes and ideas to remember

Made me want to learn more about these subjects

Book title

Author

Date started

Date finished

Genre

Rating ☆ ☆ ☆ ☆ ☆

Passages, quotes and ideas to remember

Made me want to learn more about these subjects

Book title

Author

Date started

Date finished

Genre

Rating ☆☆☆☆☆

Passages, quotes and ideas to remember

Made me want to learn more about these subjects

Book title

Author

Date started

Date finished

Genre

Rating ☆ ☆ ☆ ☆ ☆

Passages, quotes and ideas to remember

Made me want to learn more about these subjects

Book title

Author

Date started

Date finished

Genre

Rating ☆ ☆ ☆ ☆ ☆

Passages, quotes and ideas to remember

Made me want to learn more about these subjects

Book title

Author

Date started

Date finished

Genre

Rating ☆☆☆☆☆

Passages, quotes and ideas to remember

Made me want to learn more about these subjects

Book title

Author

Date started

Date finished

Genre

Rating ☆ ☆ ☆ ☆ ☆

Passages, quotes and ideas to remember

Made me want to learn more about these subjects

Book title

Author

Date started

Date finished

Genre

Rating ☆☆☆☆☆

Passages, quotes and ideas to remember

Made me want to learn more about these subjects

Book title

Author

Date started

Date finished

Genre

Rating ☆☆☆☆☆

Passages, quotes and ideas to remember

Made me want to learn more about these subjects

Book title

Author

Date started

Date finished

Genre

Rating ☆☆☆☆☆

Passages, quotes and ideas to remember

Made me want to learn more about these subjects

Book title

Author

Date started

Date finished

Genre

Rating ☆ ☆ ☆ ☆ ☆

Passages, quotes and ideas to remember

Made me want to learn more about these subjects

Book title

Author

Date started

Date finished

Genre

Rating ☆ ☆ ☆ ☆ ☆

Passages, quotes and ideas to remember

Made me want to learn more about these subjects

Book title

Author

Date started

Date finished

Genre

Rating ☆ ☆ ☆ ☆ ☆

Passages, quotes and ideas to remember

Made me want to learn more about these subjects

Book title

Author

Date started

Date finished

Genre

Rating ☆ ☆ ☆ ☆ ☆

Passages, quotes and ideas to remember

Made me want to learn more about these subjects

Book title

Author

Date started

Date finished

Genre

Rating ☆ ☆ ☆ ☆ ☆

Passages, quotes and ideas to remember

Made me want to learn more about these subjects

Book title

Author

Date started

Date finished

Genre

Rating ☆ ☆ ☆ ☆ ☆

Passages, quotes and ideas to remember

Made me want to learn more about these subjects

Book title

Author

Date started

Date finished

Genre

Rating ☆☆☆☆☆

Passages, quotes and ideas to remember

Made me want to learn more about these subjects

Book title

Author

Date started

Date finished

Genre

Rating ☆☆☆☆☆

Passages, quotes and ideas to remember

Made me want to learn more about these subjects

Book title

Author

Date started

Date finished

Genre

Rating ☆ ☆ ☆ ☆ ☆

Passages, quotes and ideas to remember

Made me want to learn more about these subjects

Book title

Author

Date started

Date finished

Genre

Rating ☆☆☆☆☆

Passages, quotes and ideas to remember

Made me want to learn more about these subjects

Book title

Author

Date started

Date finished

Genre

Rating ☆ ☆ ☆ ☆ ☆

Passages, quotes and ideas to remember

Made me want to learn more about these subjects

Book title

Author

Date started

Date finished

Genre

Rating ☆☆☆☆☆

Passages, quotes and ideas to remember

Made me want to learn more about these subjects

Book title

Author

Date started

Date finished

Genre

Rating ☆☆☆☆☆

Passages, quotes and ideas to remember

Made me want to learn more about these subjects

Book title

Author

Date started

Date finished

Genre

Rating ☆ ☆ ☆ ☆ ☆

Passages, quotes and ideas to remember

Made me want to learn more about these subjects

Book title

Author

Date started

Date finished

Genre

Rating ☆ ☆ ☆ ☆ ☆

Passages, quotes and ideas to remember

Made me want to learn more about these subjects

Book title

Author

Date started

Date finished

Genre

Rating ☆☆☆☆☆

Passages, quotes and ideas to remember

Made me want to learn more about these subjects

Book title

Author

Date started

Date finished

Genre

Rating ☆ ☆ ☆ ☆ ☆

Passages, quotes and ideas to remember

Made me want to learn more about these subjects

Book title

Author

Date started

Date finished

Genre

Rating ☆ ☆ ☆ ☆ ☆

Passages, quotes and ideas to remember

Made me want to learn more about these subjects

Book title

Author

Date started

Date finished

Genre

Rating ☆ ☆ ☆ ☆ ☆

Passages, quotes and ideas to remember

Made me want to learn more about these subjects

Book title

Author

Date started

Date finished

Genre

Rating ☆ ☆ ☆ ☆ ☆

Passages, quotes and ideas to remember

Made me want to learn more about these subjects

Book title

Author

Date started

Date finished

Genre

Rating ☆☆☆☆☆

Passages, quotes and ideas to remember

Made me want to learn more about these subjects

Book title

Author

Date started

Date finished

Genre

Rating ☆☆☆☆☆

Passages, quotes and ideas to remember

Made me want to learn more about these subjects

Book title

Author

Date started

Date finished

Genre

Rating ☆☆☆☆☆

Passages, quotes and ideas to remember

Made me want to learn more about these subjects

Book title

Author

Date started

Date finished

Genre

Rating ☆ ☆ ☆ ☆ ☆

Passages, quotes and ideas to remember

Made me want to learn more about these subjects

Book title

Author

Date started

Date finished

Genre

Rating ☆ ☆ ☆ ☆ ☆

Passages, quotes and ideas to remember

Made me want to learn more about these subjects

Book title

Author

Date started

Date finished

Genre

Rating ☆ ☆ ☆ ☆ ☆

Passages, quotes and ideas to remember

Made me want to learn more about these subjects

Book title

Author

Date started

Date finished

Genre

Rating ☆ ☆ ☆ ☆ ☆

Passages, quotes and ideas to remember

Made me want to learn more about these subjects

Book title

Author

Date started

Date finished

Genre

Rating ☆ ☆ ☆ ☆ ☆

Passages, quotes and ideas to remember

Made me want to learn more about these subjects

Book title

Author

Date started

Date finished

Genre

Rating ☆☆☆☆☆

Passages, quotes and ideas to remember

Made me want to learn more about these subjects

CPSIA information can be obtained
at www.ICGtesting.com
Printed in the USA
LVOW06s0116160917
548937LV00009B/624/P